W9-AFS-957
Mr. Kazarian
ALIEN LIBRARIAN
by Steve Foxe
illustrated by Gary Boller
STONE ARCH BOOKS
a capstone imprint

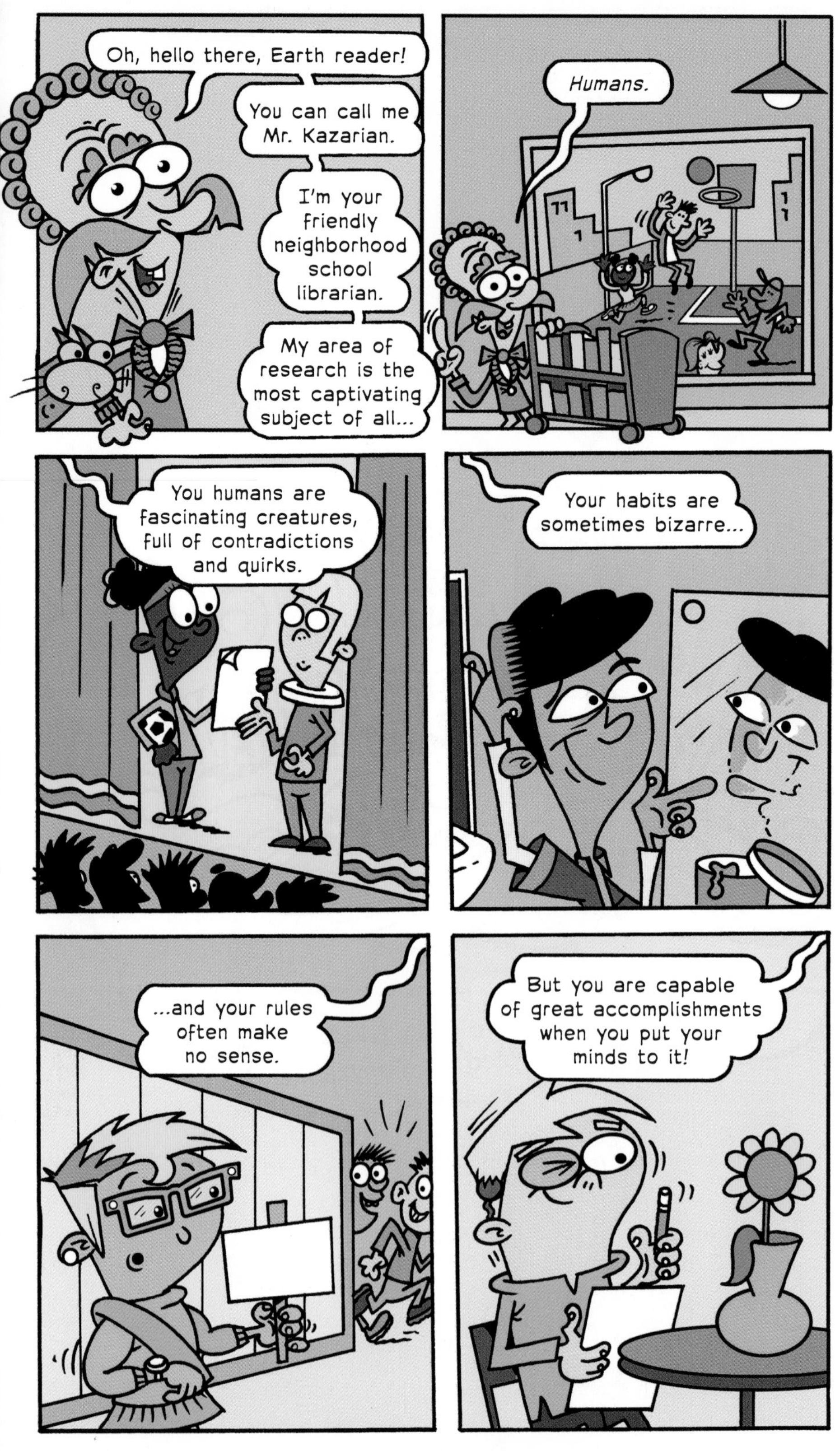
Oh, hello there, Earth reader!
You can call me Mr. Kazarian.
I'm your friendly neighborhood school librarian.
My area of research is the most captivating subject of all...
Humans.
You humans are fascinating creatures, full of contradictions and quirks.
Your habits are sometimes bizarre...
...and your rules often make no sense.
But you are capable of great accomplishments when you put your minds to it!

Oh, where are my manners? I'd lose my skorlpnox if it wasn't attached to my flumwab.
I forgot to mention that I'm not exactly from around here.
I'm more comfortable in my natural state.
RING!!!!
But Earth children expect their librarian to be a member of the human race.
I wouldn't want to scare them with my true identity.

Earlier...
Students, your research project can take any form. An essay, a song, a poem, or just about anything else, as long as it focuses on gas giants.
Yes, TJ?
My moms say it's polite to ignore gas, not focus on it.
Will your mothers also ignore the failing grade you'll receive if you don't take this assignment seriously?
DING DING DING
Try to spend some of your study period thinking about your project. It's due Monday!

TJ, maybe your research project can be a stand-up comedy routine.
You mean all these years of fart jokes might come in handy?
I think Walden is just cracking a joke of his own.
I can already imagine the super-impressive projects you guys will do...
Walden is going to paint some epic planetary artwork that Mrs. Tsao will hang on the board all year.
And Shea will turn the lesson into a Shakespearean sonnet that makes everyone break out in applause.
What about me, huh?
Whatever you do, Dani, it will be perfectly formatted and have more vocab words than Mrs. Tsao can count.

I wish. Open-ended assignments freak me out. I can never decide what to do.
Whatever I come up with, I have to do between play rehearsal, soccer practice, and piano lessons.
Everything we learned about gas giants is floating out of my brain already.
I know what we need! We need--
Mr. Kazarian!
What? No, I was going to say a pizza break.
Why would you break a pizza? I thought they were called slices. You kids and your lingo!
Now, how can I assist you four fine human beings today?

Mrs. Tsao assigned a research project on gas giants, but none of us knows where to start.
Ah, space! My *favorite* frontier. Follow me, junior astronomers.
AH-CHOO!
Behold, the books that will take you to the stars...
...and beyond!
Look who I found in my--*ah-choo!*--classroom.
Mr. Kazarian, I have three cats at home. Why is your troublemaker the only one that gives me allergies?
If I weren't such an animal lover, I'd ask the school board to--
Quark! Get back here and stop causing a commotion!
CRASH!
SMASH!
Oh dear!

Oh great. There go our expert resources.
Don't worry, Dani. You still have a whole weekend to stress about the--
CLK!
CHK-
CHK-
CHK-
CHK-

So...COOL!!!
Do you think it's full of lasers and jet packs and--
TJ! Get away from there! It looks dangerous.
CHK-
Well, this is awkward...
Are you secretly a prop designer for Hollywood?
Or a spy with cutting-edge technology?
Or an... ALIEN!?
TJ, aliens don't exist.
Sigh Actually, TJ's right, kids.
See this fashionable watch?
It's really...

...a holographic disguise projector.
Don't be alarmed, kids. I come in peace!
TAP!
Uh, what now?

My name truly is Mr. Kazarian--or that's the closest human mouths can come to pronouncing it, anyway.
SLAM!
I come from the planet Pflittlehorn, billions of light-years away.
We discovered your little corner of the universe only recently. I'm the lucky researcher chosen to study your unique species.
ZAP!
And where better to observe humans than an elementary school! Humans your age are rapidly developing your fascinating, curious behaviors.
BRICK ELEM
NO PARKING
So you're not here to take over our school and then the rest of the planet?
If this spaceship can travel superfast, does that mean you can take us to see cool space stuff up close?
I wonder how far I could kick a soccer ball in space's zero gravity...
Oh my yorgblerg, I should say not! I'm not cut out for conquest.

Hmm, you *do* have 45 minutes left until your next class.
That's enough time to see the gas giants, I'd say. For research purposes, of course.
Do we need permission slips from our parents?
The fewer humans who find out who I am, the better. They might send me home--or worse! It's extremely important that I finish my research and share it with the youth of Pflittlehorn.
It's like they're forgetting how to be kids! I've got to find out where we're going wrong...
But being a kid is the best! Don't worry, Mr. K, we won't tell anyone about your spaceship.
In that case, I think an up-close-and-personal lesson on gas giants is the least I can do.
Buckle up, children.

Here... we...
ZOOOOOM!
GO!
TJ... are you... chewing gum... during launch?
It relieves... my stress!
Oops, should have mentioned--it can get a bit bumpy leaving Earth's atmosphere.
Welcome, kids, to the fifth planet from the sun...

...JUPITER!
What is it you kids always say? "Go big or go home"?
Is this big enough for you? Jupiter is by far the largest planet in your solar system.
It's massive!
Yes, it does contain mass. Good observation, Shea! Of course, there is a difference between size and mass.
When I say biggest, I mean the distance from one side of the planet straight through to the other side--the diameter.

Jupiter has a diameter of almost 143,000 kilometers. That's like 11 Earths stacked side by side!
Mass is sort of like a planet's weight. Jupiter is as massive as 318 planet Earths combined.
Jupiter is named for the ancient Roman king of the gods.
I believe modern Earthlings are more familiar with his Greek name: Zeus!

Are we going to land on the surface?
Land on *what* surface? I don't see much down there...
We call Jupiter a *gas giant* because it's mostly made up of elements like hydrogen and helium.
Up to 90 percent of the planet is gas and liquid, with a small metallic core.
So, it's like a giant swimming pool?
A giant swimming pool with a magnetic field 20,000 times stronger than Earth's!

And some of its winds blow more than 600 kilometers per hour!
Not to mention that Jupiter rotates very quickly--about once every 10 Earth hours.
But its *orbit* is much slower.
It takes Jupiter almost 12 Earth years to make one full trip around the sun.

What about Jupiter's moons? I was thinking of making a diorama for my project.
You'll need a lot of foam balls for that, Walden. Scientists believe Jupiter has 79 moons!
(Pflittlehorn has 142, but who's counting?)
The great Earth astronomer Galileo Galilei discovered Jupiter's four largest moons back in 1610.
Ganymede isn't just Jupiter's biggest moon--it's the largest satellite in your galaxy!
It's even larger than Mercury or Pluto. It would be considered a planet if it orbited the sun instead of Jupiter.
Ganymede
Pluto
Mercury

Io is the most volcanically active moon or planet in your solar system.
Its surface looks a bit like a certain Earth food...
(Reminds me of the great cheese oceans of Pflittlehorn...)
Callisto is sometimes called the "dead moon" because the surface is dark and doesn't seem to change. But Callisto may be home to a vast underground ocean!
We know for sure that the moon Europa is covered in frozen water. Human scientists are planning an unmanned mission to Europa to see if its oceans can support life.
(We Pflittlehornians already investigated, but I won't spoil the surprise for you.)

My dad always says I'm a visual learner, but that's a lot of visuals to take in...
We're just getting started, Walden! Why, Jupiter's cloud layers alone--
Uhh...Mr. K, what's that giant red swirly spot?
It looks pretty dangerous, and we're getting closer to it...
Ah, the Great Red Spot!
A storm large enough to fit planet Earth inside it.
The Great Red Spot has been raging for more than 300 years.

Don't fret, Dani! My intergalactic piloting license record is SPOTless. We'll steer far clear of--
Me-OWWW!
Looks like we've got a stowaway stray!
Quark, you frumgupious feline! Come here before you cause any trouble.
BOiNG!
Too late!
Quark, no!
BZZZZZ-AP
BEEP! BEEP!
CLK-CLK

LURCH!
How's that stress-relief gum working for you?
Like a charm.
No permission slip on Earth could cover this!
Don't worry, kids! They don't call me Quick-Eye Kazarian for nothing.
(Well, no one actually calls me that, but I've been trying to get that nickname to catch on....)
Hold... on... tight...

Did I say my intergalactic piloting license record was SPOTless?
Because it looks like we're headed for one very big *spot*.
Wait Mr. K! I think Walden and I can help!
Your steering-orb-thingie looks like a soccer ball. No one is better at handling a soccer ball than I am!
How can *I* help?
Give the cat to Dani and be my spotter! You've got the attention to detail that we need to get out of here.
A *spot* spotter?
I do encourage hands-on learning...
I'll control the stabilizers while you take the lead!

Watch out on your left!
Here goes nothing...
gulp
We're going to be space roadkill! And there aren't even roads in space!

Yeowl!
You're doing it, Shea! Almost there!
Goal!
A bit to the right!

Well done, young Shea! Our autopilot can steer us safely now.
I couldn't have done it better myself!
Thanks, TJ! I'm just glad none of your gum got in *my* hair.
Bah, foul substance! On my planet, chewing gum is a punishment for our worst criminals.
I'd take that punishment any day!
bleargh
Should we take Quark back to the library before our next stop, Mr. K?
Not necessary. This magneto-collar will keep Quark from getting within 24 dorgnocks of the navigation console.

hmpf
Now if you'll all take your seats, we can head for the next gas giant on our trip.
We might have a chance to get a little more hands-on for this one.
More hands-on?
Say goodbye to Jupiter...

...and hello
to Saturn!
Those rings
are beautiful.
It's so different
from Jupiter.

Actually, Saturn and Jupiter are quite similar.
Both planets are made up mostly of the same elements, and both rotate at high speeds.
Most humans think Saturn is the only planet with rings. But Jupiter, Uranus, and Neptune all have rings as well.
Saturn's rings are just more spectacular!
Jupiter and Saturn are practically family--Saturn was named after Jupiter's father in Roman mythology.
Aww.

But enough of my lecture. Who wants to explore Saturn's rings up close and--
I volunteer!
There's no rush! I have enough S.U.R.F. suits to go around.
S.U.R.F. suits?
Dani, you're a safety officer at school, right?
Will you help demonstrate how the S.U.R.F. suit works?
As long as it's not as intense as getting out of the Great Red Spot.
Not at all! It's as simple as...
BOOP!

S.U.R.F. stands for Space Uniform Radiance Field.
It recycles breathable air and regulates the temperature.
Each helmet creates a force field that conforms to the wearer's body--whether they have arms, wings, flippers, tentacles, or squibfongs.
Will it work with my hearing aid?
Of course, Walden! The S.U.R.F. suit will also allow us to communicate with each other in the vacuum of space.
What if we accidentally press the button while we're out in space?
The S.U.R.F. suit will only turn off if it detects a safe environment. And each one has a tracker in case you stray too far from the ship.

I'll set the ship to autopilot and you can space-board while we learn more about Saturn!
I prefer to space-ski, myself. Space-boarding is for younger knees.
I believe the Earth saying is "Hang 10," everyone!
Woo-hoo!

Saturn's rings are made up of billions of pieces of ice, dust, and rock. The pieces are probably from asteroids, comets, and even moons that broke up in Saturn's gravity.
Some particles are as small as a grain of sand. Others are bigger than an Earthling's home!
The rings spread up to 400,000 kilometers from the planet but are only about 10 meters thick. That's about 33 feet.
(I wonder why humans measure things in feet. Pflittlehornians don't measure things in tentacles...)
Saturn looks pale yellow to us from here because its upper atmosphere is full of ammonia crystals.
In fact, Saturn is one of five planets humans can see from Earth without the help of a telescope. Mercury, Venus, Mars, and Jupiter are the others.

Is anyone listening to my fascinating Saturn facts?
Of course, Mr. K! We're just enjoying this once-in-a-lifetime experience too!
Ah yes, I forget that not all species spend their youthful years on interstellar ski trips.
If you tire of space-boarding the rings, Saturn has 62 known moons to explore too. All of them frozen.
Saturn's largest moon, Titan, has its own atmosphere. That's highly unusual for a moon.
Some Earth scientists even suspect that unusual life-forms may be living in Titan's liquid methane lakes!

Is Saturn bigger than Earth?
Oh my, yes. In fact, Saturn and Jupiter combined make up 92 percent of planetary mass in your solar system.
But that's not all: Saturn is also the least *dense* planet.
If you filled the biggest bathtub in the universe with water, Saturn would float like a beach ball!
Saturn could enjoy a long, relaxing bath too. Its orbit around the sun takes almost 30 Earth years.
It takes so long to orbit because Saturn is just short of 1.5 *billion* kilometers away from the sun.
By comparison, your planet is only about 150 *million* kilometers from the sun.

Are we going to get any closer to the planet?
Saturn's winds might be a little strong for our S.U.R.F. suits.
At about 1,800 kilometers per hour, they're some of the fastest known winds in your solar system. Only Neptune's winds are faster.
Saturn's rotation is quite fast too--about 10.5 Earth hours.
If Earth's days were only 10.5 hours, your recess would be just a few minutes long!
That fast rotation combined with low density gives Saturn a slightly oval shape. It's actually the flattest planet in your solar system.

Ready to return to the ship, my fearless space-boarders?
Aww, already?
I just started learning some tricks!
Pflittlehornians have very keen senses of smell. If you kids get too worked up out here, my ship will smell like one of your locker rooms.
And trust someone who's been all over the universe: Almost nothing smells as bad as Earth child locker rooms.
Besides, you've already learned so much about your system's gas giants.
Wouldn't you like to explore the *ice* giants, as well?
Awesome! My cat scarf will keep me warm!

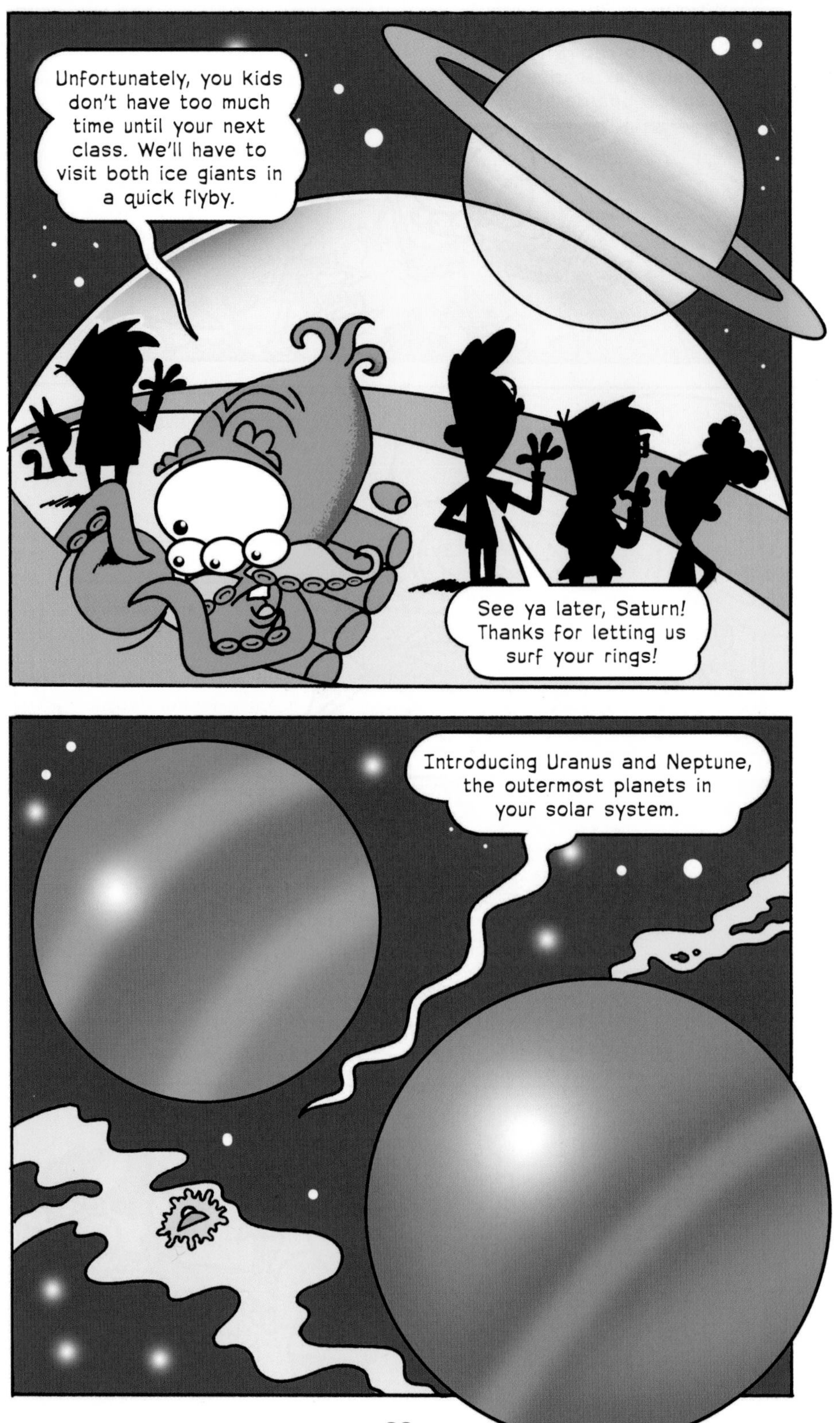
Unfortunately, you kids don't have too much time until your next class. We'll have to visit both ice giants in a quick flyby.
See ya later, Saturn! Thanks for letting us surf your rings!
Introducing Uranus and Neptune, the outermost planets in your solar system.

I thought ice giants were those big blue bad guys that Thor fights in Norse mythology?
Don't think of the word *ice* so literally.
These planets are called ice giants because they're mostly made up of heavier elements than the gas giant elements.
Ice giants are full of oxygen, carbon, and sulfur.
Those elements were probably solid ice, or gasses trapped in ice, when the planets first formed.
There's a lot of information that Earth scientists are still figuring out about ice giants.

Uranus was discovered in the 1700s. After much debate, astronomers named it after the Greek version of Saturn's father.
Uranus
Saturn
Jupiter
Generations of planets, one after the other!
One of the most striking things about Uranus is its dramatic tilt.
It's likely that something large ran into it not long after it formed.
(I swear, I didn't hit it with my ship.)
Now it spins around the sun at such an angle that each half of the planet faces the sun for about 21 Earth years at a time!
Even so, Uranus is the coldest planet in the solar system for all 84 Earth years of its orbit. It produces very little heat.

Brrr, sounds like Uranus is the last place you'd want to visit.
It's truly a unique planet!
It has weather conditions that cause carbon and hydrogen to squeeze together in the atmosphere, making it rain diamonds!
Ah yes, I always forget that humans value diamonds. Such a strange obsession--you can't even eat them!
Diamonds!
Now, let's zoom past Neptune and we'll get back before the bell rings.
Uh, Mr. K?
Is that where Quark's litter box is kept?
No, that's the emergency feline escape portal. Why do you ask?

Uhh...
Quark! That darn cat could get lost forever out here. We're 3 billion kilometers away from Earth!
I'll go get him, Mr. K!
I was the one who thought it was his litter box, after all.
It's not your fault, Walden.
But Quark has taken a liking to you...
We'll both go.
Dani, Shea, TJ-- don't touch the autopilot. We'll be right back with that cat.
Wait! Cats always wiggle loose. My gum will stick to his suit so he can't get away from you.
gag

You go right, I'll go left.
Right is the same as siggleborp, right? Pflittlehornians have more directions than you do.
Here, kitty, kitty. Let's go back in the nice, safe spaceship.
Almost had him!
Oh no, look! A comet is heading straight for them!
We have to warn them!
Mr. Kazarian! Walden! Look behind you!

ZAP!
KABLAMM!
LASER CAT! LASER CAT!
Gotcha!
LASER CAT!
LASER CAT!

I suppose I should have explained--Quark isn't an Earth cat, he's a *Pflittlehornian* cat.
Pflittlehornian cats just happen to look exactly like Earth cats. It's a one-in-a-quintillion cosmic coincidence, really!
Is that why Mrs. Tsao is allergic to Quark but not other cats?
Without a doubt! I try to keep Quark out of trouble, but Pflittlehornian cats have minds of their own.
And that's different from Earth cats how?
I've disabled the exits Quark could use on his own, so we're free to finish a quick tour of Neptune.
Thank you for your assistance, Walden. You should know that Pflittlehornian cats are very loyal once they bond with another life-form.
I *knew* my chewing gum would come in handy.
ZAP!

Neptune is named for the Roman god of the seas.
Only one Earth craft has visited Neptune, way back in 1989. So most of what your species has observed about the planet has required powerful telescopes.
However! Neptune was actually the first planet humans discovered with math.
A French astronomer named Alexis Bouvard had a theory that a nearby planet was affecting Uranus's orbit.
Math for the win!
That led a German astronomer named Johann Galle to find its neighbor Neptune with a telescope and some *very* complex calculations!
Neptune's rocky core is thought to be about the size of Earth. Around that core is a slushy mix of water, methane, and ammonia ices.

Neptune has an average distance from the sun of 4.5 billion kilometers.
In fact, Neptune has only completed ONE orbit since its discovery. It takes 165 Earth years to make the full journey.
Weee!
Pluto's orbit crosses with Neptune's every 250 Earth years or so. During that time Pluto is actually closer to the sun than Neptune.
PLUTO
But Pluto isn't even a planet anymore!
Correct! It was reclassified as a dwarf planet in 2006. That means Neptune is always the farthest *planet* from the sun.
Sorry, Pluto.
Neptune has 14 known moons, including Triton.
Triton is the only large moon in your solar system that orbits its planet in the opposite direction of its planet's rotation.
Scientists think Triton orbits that way because it was a dwarf planet that Neptune captured!

See ya later, Neptune! It's time for us to return to Earth.
BEEP BEEP!
Aww!
Don't worry, children. There's a whole galaxy's worth of knowledge waiting for you back at the library too!

Best. Field. Trip. Ever.
Do you think learning to snowboard would be as cool as space-boarding?
Definitely less chance of getting hit by an asteroid!
Ah-*choo!*
Walden, how can you--*ah-choo!*--hold that beast without--*ah-choo!*--sneezing?
I am allergic to most cats, but not this one. Right, laser buddy?
Laser buddy? And what's this green fog everywhere?
Sorry, Mrs. T. Cafeteria burritos can turn anyone into a gas giant.
You know what? I'm just happy you--*ah-choo!*--remember what we studied in class today.

I trust that Mr. Kazarian has--*ah-choo!*--helped you all decide on your research projects, due Monday, you recall?
You know it! I just wish we had taken pictures of the gas gia--
Pictures of...the gas giant *websites* we're going to look up at home.
So we don't forget the URLs.
sniff
Yes, well, I'm going back to my classroom before my nose runs off my face.
You children have a lovely and productive weekend. You too, Mr. Kazarian. Thank you for--*ah-choo!*--helping them with their research.
Fast thinking, Dani!
Thanks, Mr. K. But that was too close for comfort. What if we slip up and say something about you being an alien?
Yeah, and then the government shows up to kidnap you for top secret research, and we all have to go on the run as fugitives to protect you!

Maybe take it down a notch, TJ.
Don't worry, kids. Let me talk to Quark for a moment and we'll come up with a solution.
Quark can *talk!?*
Of course. Can't Earth cats? I assumed they were just snooty.
At any rate, I believe we can fix this.
Just look into Quark's eyes for a moment...
FLSHH!

Whoa, did you make us forget all the cool library adventures we had in outer library?
Wait, why do I keep saying "library" when I'm trying to say "library?"
I asked Quark to implant a secret word swapper! Whenever you accidentally start to say that I'm an alien from outer space, your brain will automatically change your words for you.
You're "a librarian!"
From the "library!"
With an "amazing, flawless, perfect" cat. Hey, wait a minute.
Hmm, Quark might have added a few extra word swaps of his own...
DING DING DING!
Aww, I can't believe we have to go back to class after such an amazing trip through "the library."
If you can have this much fun in "the library," imagine how much fun you might have in your other classes!
Yeah, who knows-- maybe every teacher has a secret bookshelf!

A few days later...
Research log number #12,789:
Despite serving as an educator here on Earth, I feel that I'm learning as much from my students as they're learning from me.
Not only do these Earth children thrive during challenges--they volunteer for them to help those in need.
They put others before themselves and have a strong sense of responsibility.
Earth children are quick, clever, and often wise beyond their years.
Even the practical jokers among them are creative thinkers, eager to help however they can.

But perhaps even more important to my research, human children have a healthy sense of awe and wonder about the world around them.
I suspect Pflittlehornian children have become bored after eons of universal knowledge at their tentacle-tips.
Maybe we expect Pflittlehornians to grow up too fast. There's so much joy to be had during our youthful years!
As the wise TJ said, perhaps it is time that we, as a species, "break the pizza" and remember how to have fun.

Most Earth children may never travel through space like the average Pflittlehornian. But it is clear that their imaginations can still reach the stars.
If these Earthlings have taught me anything, it's that life is all about balance. Study along with play, logic with wonder, learning with... fart jokes.
What wonders have we been ignoring right on Pflittlehorn as we seek to discover the far reaches of the universe?
I sense that my studies of--no, my studies *with*--these children are far from over.

They clearly have much left to teach me...
Before I begin, I just want to thank Mr. Kazarian the librarian for all his help on this research project.
I couldn't have done it without him.

Well Quark, I think that's enough for now. The Pflittlehornian Science Council will be glad to have an update on my mission.
Oh my! You kids startled me. Good thing it was you!
How did your research projects on gas giants go?
Oh, they went great, Mr. K! We all got As.
I got an A plus!
But we were wondering...
Mrs. Tsao assigned another space research project, and all of us have a free period for the next hour, so...
The learning continues!

More About Gas Giants

These four planets were once known as Gas Giants, but Uranus and Neptune were later classified as Ice Giants.

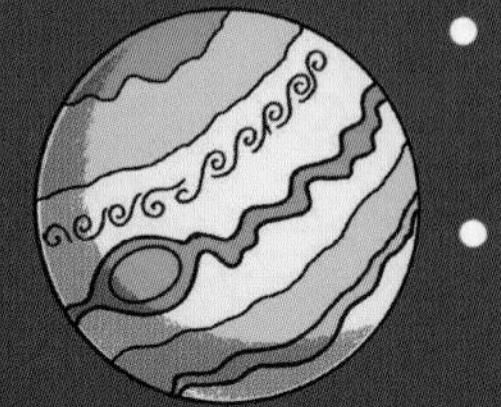

Composition: 90% hydrogen, 10% helium, with small amounts of ammonia, sulfur, methane, and water vapor
Diameter: 142,984 km
Mass: 1.9 × 1,027 kg (318 x Earth's mass)
Distance from the Sun: 778.5 million km
Orbit Period: 11.9 years

SATURN

6th Planet from the Sun

Composition: 96.3% hydrogen, 3.25% helium, with small amounts of methane and ammonia
Diameter: 115,873 km
Mass: 5.683 × 1,026 kg (95 x Earth's mass)
Distance from the Sun: 1.4 billion km
Orbit Period: 29.5 years

Mr. Kazarian, Alien Librarian is published by Stone Arch Books,
a Capstone Imprint
1710 Roe Crest Drive
North Mankato, Minnesota 56003
www.capstonepub.com

Library of Congress Cataloging-in-Publication Data
Names: Foxe, Steve, author. | Boller, Gary, illustrator.
Title: Mr. Kazarian, alien librarian / by Steve Foxe ; illustrated by Gary Boller.
Description: North Mankato, Minnesota : Stone Arch Books, a Capstone Imprint, [2020] | Series: Mr. Kazarian, alien librarian ; 1 | Summary: Mr. Kazarian, the school librarian, is actually an extraterrestrial (with a holographic disguise) studying the behavior of human children, and if he wants to continue his research he will have to find a way to convince the four students who have discovered his secret not to expose him—perhaps by helping their assignment on gas giants with a quick trip to space.
Identifiers: LCCN 2018054841 (print) | LCCN 2018057513 (ebook) | ISBN 9781496583710 (ebook PDF) | ISBN 9781496583666 (hardcover) | ISBN 9781496593412 (paperback)
Subjects: LCSH: Extraterrestrial beings—Comic books, strips, etc. | Extraterrestrial beings—Juvenile fiction. | Librarians—Comic books, strips, etc. | Librarians—Juvenile fiction. | School field trips—Comic books, strips, etc. | School field trips—Juvenile fiction. | Graphic novels. | Jupiter (Planet)—Comic books, strips, etc. | Jupiter (Planet)—Juvenile fiction. | CYAC: Graphic novels. | Extraterrestrial Beings—Fiction. | Librarians—Fiction. | School field trips—Fiction. | Jupiter (Planet)—Fiction. | LCGFT: Graphic novels.
Classification: LCC PZ7.1.F694 (ebook) | LCC PZ7.7.F69 Mr 2020 (print) | DDC 741.5/973—dc23
LC record available at https://lccn.loc.gov/2018054841

Editorial Credits
Kristen Mohn, editor; Ted Williams, designer; Kelly Garvin, media researcher; Tori Abraham, production specialist

Printed in the United States of America.
PA99

Steve

Steve Foxe is the author of more than 20 children's books and comics for properties including Pokémon, Transformers, Adventure Time, Steven Universe, DC Super Friends, and Grumpy Cat. He is the editor of *Paste* magazine's comic section and lives in Queens, New York, where he thinks a lot about cats, even ones who can't shoot lasers from their eyes.

Gary

Gary Boller is an illustrator and animator based in London. He has written and illustrated many children's books and comics, including strips for *The Beano, The Dandy,* and *The Times*. He also works in advertising and entertainment, including the Bafta winning animated series, The Amazing Adrenalini Brothers. Gary, too, is never very far away from a cat and is unwittingly helping them take control of this planet.

Read More

Baker, Theo. *Gas Giant Jump*. Galaxy Games. Vero Beach, FL: Rourke Educational Media, 2017.

Cruddas, Sarah. *Solar System*. DKfindout! New York: DK Publishing, 2016.

Radomski, Kassandra. *The Secrets of Saturn*. Planets. North Mankato, MN: Capstone Press, 2015.

Spilsbury, Richard. *Space*. Adventures in STEAM. North Mankato, MN: Capstone Press, 2018.

Deep Thoughts with Mr. Kazarian

This story combines fiction (made-up) and nonfiction (true) elements. What are two true things you learned about planets from this story?

- Each of the four kids in the story has his or her own interests and hobbies. Can you name one fact each about TJ, Shea, Walden, and Dani?
- Mr. Kazarian works as a librarian on Earth. What qualities do you think a great librarian should have?
- Mrs. Tsao, the science teacher, assigns a research project on gas giants. What kind of project would you make to show what you learned about gas giants?
- Mr. Kazarian comes from a fictional alien planet. If you created a made-up planet, what would it look like and what kind of aliens would live there?

Glossary

ammonia—a smelly, colorless gas that is a compound of nitrogen and hydrogen

carbon—a chemical element, found in all living things, that is the basis for life

density—the relationship of an object's mass to its volume

dwarf planet—a celestial body that orbits the sun and has a round shape but is not large enough to affect other objects in orbit

element—a substance that cannot be broken down into simpler substances

galaxy—a cluster of millions of stars bound together by gravity

gas giant—a large planet of relatively low density made mostly of hydrogen and helium; Saturn and Jupiter are gas giants

helium—a lightweight, colorless gas that does not burn

hydrogen—a colorless gas that is lighter than air and burns easily

ice giant—a large planet made mainly of substances that are heavier than helium and hydrogen; Uranus and Neptune are ice giants

kilometer—a metric unit of measurement equal to 1,000 meters, or approximately 0.62 miles

methane—a colorless, flammable gas; methane becomes a liquid at extremely cold temperatures

orbit—the path an object follows as it goes around the sun or a planet

oxygen—a colorless gas that people breathe; humans and animals need oxygen to live

rotation—the motion of an object around an internal axis

satellite—an object in space that circles a larger object, such as a planet

sulfur—a yellow chemical element that burns easily and is very smelly

and Ice Giants

URANUS

7th Planet from the Sun

Composition: 83% hydrogen, 15% helium, and 2% methane, with a molten core
Diameter: 50,724 km
Mass: 8.681 × 1,025 kg (14.5 x Earth's mass)
Distance from the Sun: 2.8 billion km
Orbit Period: 84.0 years

NEPTUNE

8th Planet from the Sun

Composition: About 80% hydrogen and 19% helium, with a small amount of water and methane
Diameter: 49,244 km
Mass: 1.024 × 1,026 kg (17 x Earth's mass)
Distance from the Sun: 4.5 billion km
Orbit Period: 165 years